nosy
crow

EVERY BUNNY
is a
YOGA BUNNY

Emily Ann Davison
&
Deborah Allwright

Yo-Yo was a fidgety bunny.

A bouncy bunny.

A can't-sit-still-**ever** type of bunny.

She tried her best . . .

EVERY BUNNY
is a
YO NY

First published in 2022 by Nosy Crow Ltd
The Crow's Nest, 14 Baden Place, Crosby Row, London, SE1 1YW, UK

Nosy Crow Eireann Ltd
44 Orchard Grove, Kenmare, Co Kerry, V93 FY22, Ireland

www.nosycrow.com

ISBN 978 1 83994 067 5 (HB)
ISBN 978 1 83994 068 2 (PB)

A CIP catalogue record for this book is available from the British Library.

Printed in China

Papers used by Nosy Crow are made from wood grown in sustainable forests.

10 9 8 7 6 5 4 3 2 1 (HB)
10 9 8 7 6 5 4 3 2 (PB)

For Dad and Rosie,
with love always
E.A.D.

For Juno
D.A.

but her legs were too **jiggly.**

Her bottom was too **wiggly.**

And Yo-Yo was just too **giggly.**

Every night, Grandpa tucked Yo-Yo
and the other little bunnies into bed.

Roly and Flo were soon fast asleep . . .

but Yo-Yo jiggled and wiggled . . .
and rolled out of bed.
"Whoops!" she giggled.

"Calm down, Yo-Yo," said Grandpa.

"But I don't feel calm," said Yo-Yo.

"Oh, Yo-Yo. I wonder what
we can do to help."

The next day, Grandpa had an idea.
"Today, little bunnies, we're going to do yoga," he said.

"What's that?" asked Flo.

"Yoga is a way to help you feel calm by breathing slowly and stretching into different shapes," said Grandpa.

"First, let's crouch down like a frog on a log. Breathe in. And out. And in. And out."

Yo-Yo tried very, very hard, but the prickly grass . . .

tickled her bottom. "Ha ha ha!" giggled Yo-Yo.

"Oh, Yo-Yo!" said Grandpa.

"Next, little bunnies, lie down and push your bottoms up. Imagine a stream flowing under you," said Grandpa. "Breathe in. And out. And in. And out.

There! You all look like little bridges."

But Yo-Yo waggled her legs in the air.
"Look, Roly! Let's pretend we're splashing in the stream!"

"Oh, Yo-Yo!" said Roly.

"Now, the next one is easy," said Grandpa.
"Stand up strong and still like a mountain.
Close your eyes. Breathe in. And out.
And in. And out."

Roly could stand up strong and still like a mountain. So could Flo.

But Yo-Yo jiggled and wiggled.

"Oh, Yo-Yo!" said Flo.

"Now, can you place one foot on your other ankle?" said Grandpa. "Stretch your arms up like branches on a **tree.**"

Grandpa and Roly and Flo stretched up tall like trees. They breathed in. And out. And in. And out.

But just then . . .

Yo-Yo spotted something colourful.
It fluttered up. And down.
And up. And down.

She simply **had** to take a closer look . . .

Yo-Yo **twirled** past a tall tree . . .

marched down a mountain . . .

bounded across a bridge . . .

and leapt over a log . . .

all the way to . . .

...a deep,

dark,

shadowy forest.

Yo-Yo **huffed**
and **puffed** in a panic.

Thoughts **whizzed**
around in her mind.

Her tummy **flipped** inside.

And she suddenly felt **very lost.**

Yo-Yo flopped to the floor,
when something . . .

. . . tickled her bottom. It was prickly grass!

"Oooh! I'm crouching like a frog on a log, just like Grandpa taught me," said Yo-Yo.

She breathed in. And out. And in. And out. Slowly, her breath stopped huffing and puffing.

"I leapt over the log before I got lost!" remembered Yo-Yo.

"But what yoga shape did
Grandpa make next?" she said.
"I know! The **bridge!**"

Yo-Yo lay down and pushed her bottom up like a bridge.

She breathed in. And out.
And in. And out.

Slowly, her thoughts stopped whizzing around.
She imagined a stream flowing underneath her.
"The stream!" remembered Yo-Yo.
"I bounded across the bridge, over the stream!"

"What yoga shape did we make next?" said Yo-Yo.
"I know! The **mountain**!"

Yo-Yo stood up strong and still like a mountain.
She breathed in. And out. And in. And out.
Slowly, her tummy stopped flipping inside.

"I marched down the mountain!"
remembered Yo-Yo.

"Now, what did we do next?" she said.
"I know! The tree!"

Then Yo-Yo stretched up tall like a tree.
She breathed in. And out. And in. And out.
And suddenly, she didn't feel so lost.

"I twirled past the tall tree!"
remembered Yo-Yo.

"I know the way home!"

Yo-Yo **leapt** over the log . . .

bounded across the bridge . . .

marched up the mountain . . .

and twirled past the tall tree . . .

all the way . . .

. . . **home,** to the other bunnies,
who were **still** doing yoga.

Grandpa and Roly and Flo were sitting down
with their legs crossed and their eyes closed.
They breathed in. And out. And in. And out.

Yo-Yo sat down too.
This time, she stayed **very** still.

"There you are, Yo-Yo," said Grandpa.

Yo-Yo closed her eyes and smiled.
"Feeling calm isn't so tricky after all," she said.

Yo-Yo was still a fidgety bunny.
A bouncy bunny.
A can't-sit-still-ever type of bunny.

But when she felt too jiggly, too wiggly,
too giggly, well . . .

Yo-Yo knew yoga would
help her to feel calm.

Goodnight,
little yoga bunnies.

Why don't you try these yoga shapes, just like Yo-Yo?

FROG
(known as Squat Pose)

BRIDGE

- Stand with your feet apart.
- Breathe in as you crouch down like a frog on a log.
- Press the palms of your hands together.
- Breathe out.

- Lie on your back with your knees bent.
- Keep your arms flat on the floor, hands palm down, stretching your fingers towards your heels.
- Breathe in and lift your bottom upwards.
- Breathe out and imagine a stream flowing underneath you.

MOUNTAIN

- Stand with your feet slightly apart and rest your arms by your sides, turning the palms of your hands to face forward.

- Pull your tummy in, and roll your shoulders back and down. Let the top of your head reach towards the sky.

- Stand strong and still like a mountain. Close your eyes, if you like. Think about each part of your body and how it feels.

- Breathe in. Breathe out.

TREE

- Stand with your feet together.

- Turn your left knee out to the left side.

- Place your left heel against the side of your right ankle. Try your best not to wobble.

- Breathe in as you stretch your arms up like branches on a tree.

- Breathe out as you bring them back down and put your palms together.

- Now repeat with your right leg.

SITTING

(known as Easy Pose)

CURL INTO YOUR BURROW

(known as Child's Pose)

- Sit down.

- Cross your legs.

- Rest your hands somewhere comfortable like the tops of your knees.

- Close your eyes, if you like.

- Sit still like a yoga bunny.

- Breathe in slowly. And out slowly.

- Come onto your hands and knees.

- Stretch your arms forward and bring your bottom down onto your heels.

- Rest your head on the floor.

- Now bring your arms back to rest next to your sides, with the palms of your hands facing up.

- Take a big breath in . . . and let it out.